GOD, I I
KNOW YOUR NAME

NEW LOVERS is a series devoted to
publishing new works of erotica
that explore the complexities
bedevilling contemporary
life, culture, and
art today.

OTHER TITLES IN THE SERIES
How To Train Your Virgin
We Love Lucy

GOD, I DON'T EVEN KNOW YOUR NAME

×

ANDREA MCGINTY

BADLANDS UNLIMITED
NEW LOVERS
Nº3

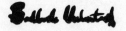

God, I Don't Even Know Your Name
by Andrea McGinty

New Lovers No.3

Published by:
Badlands Unlimited
P.O. Box 320310
Brooklyn, NY 11232
Tel: +1 718 788 6668
operator@badlandsunlimited.com
www.badlandsunlimited.com

Series editors: Paul Chan, Ian Cheng, Micaela Durand, Matthew So
Consulting editor: Karen Marta
Copy editor: Charlotte Carter
Editorial assistant: Jessica Jackson
Ebook designer: Ian Cheng
Front cover design by Kobi Benzari
Endpaper art by Paul Chan
Additional photos by Andrea McGinty
Special thanks to Luke Brown, Alex Galan, Martha Fleming-Ives, Elisa
Leshowitz, Marlo Poras, Cassie Raihl, David Torrone

Paper book distributed in the Americas by:
ARTBOOK | D.A.P. USA
155 6th Avenue, 2nd Floor
New York, NY 10013
Tel. +1 800 338 BOOK
www.artbook.com

Paper book distributed in Europe by:
Buchhandlung Walther König
Ehrenstrasse 4
50672 Köln
www.buchhandlung-walther-koenig.de

Printed in the United States of America

ISBN: 978-1-936440-86-3
E-Book ISBN: 978-1-936440-87-0

www.badlandsunlimited.com

THE TWELVE PROMISES

I: Find A Higher Happiness   1

II: Embrace The Detours In Life   5

III: Break With The Past But Don't Shut It Out   19

IV: Touch Others Like You Want To Be Touched   27

V: Find The Strength To *Know* Yourself   41

VI: Thrive In The Unknown   55

VII: Confront The Fears That Define You   61

VIII: Take The Time To Enjoy Being *Here*   73

IX: Change Your Outlook And The Rest Will Follow   81

X: Imagine A Fuller Fundament   87

XI: Create The Serenity From Within   99

XII: Master The Moment   103

About the Author   116

I

FIND A
HIGHER HAPPINESS

Dear The Universe, Jesus Christ Almighty, thank you Lord and Light for Nordic boys who speak English with a British accent on top of their own. On top of their rolling r's and drawn out vowels. On top of their translation errors and deep stares.

Thank you for that year he spent living in London.

Thank you for waking me up to find him

watching me sleep.

I have only you to thank, my Lord. Only you to thank for helping him find the perfect pressure with which to rub on my swollen clit. Not too rough, not too sweet. Only you to thank for guiding my finger gently into his asshole, so that when he came on my face he came extra hard.

From my temple to my chin.

From my ear to my pouty little lips.

Just far enough to taste his sour saltiness before licking it all off.

Because of your divine intervention we found each other at that bar. Without your guiding force I wouldn't have gone back to his flat at four in the morning so we could fuck atop that black, faux-satin duvet cover. Without you, I would never have ended up under those dirty sheets that were soaked in his musky and sweet cum, drifting off to sleep as he mumbled fuck drunk and drunk drunk nothings into my ear.

They say that God will do for you what you can't do for yourself, which I guess in this case means that I can't wake myself up in the morning by sliding my own fingers across my ass and in between my legs into my wetness while biting my ear and my neck and smelling my hair until letting out a soft cry and settling back into my own naked body.

They also say that God won't give you any more than you can handle, and I guess in this case that means his throbbing, glorious cock.

I had a vision, an almighty vision, dear God. I saw him begging me to turn over so he could take me from behind, and because of your all-seeing, all-knowing, all-loving heart, that's exactly what he did. Life truly wouldn't be worth living if a boy couldn't stick a thumb into my mouth so I can suck it while he looks deep into my eyes and pounds me harder and faster until he's good and ready and then decides to flip me over by grabbing a fistful of my hair.

As soon as I let your love into my heart, The Universe opened up to me just like I opened up to him. Wider. And Wider.

I turn my will and my life over to you, dear God, to do with my pussy what Thou wilt.

II

EMBRACE THE DETOURS IN LIFE

The hotel bar smelled like beer, which reminded Eva of what Aabel smelled like the first night she sucked his dick. It took a long time for him to come, and she realized it was because he was drunker than he let on. Eva didn't typically have patience for what she called whiskey dick, even less so now that she didn't drink. But his was of the favorable kind. Better a hard-on that won't quit than one that won't fuck.

Besides, he was different. Sitting at the bar sipping a Virgin Bloody Mary, Eva closed her eyes and pictured Aabel's boyish, dimpled face and his sexy, well-groomed beard. How long had it been since they first met? How long had it been since they first fell into bed together? Since they said their last goodbye?

She met him at that bar. Eva was in London for a week before heading to an arts residency in the Finnish countryside. She was with her friend Fawn, who was also an artist. And Fawn knew Aabel because he curated a friend of hers in an exhibition at the Serpentine Gallery. After the show opened and the afterparty ended, they all went out for one last drink.

Aabel suggested the bar at the hotel

where Eva was staying because it boasted a jukebox that only played Finnish pop songs, one of his obsessions. As Aabel and Eva danced, he translated the lyrics.

"This one's about drinking too much and it's fun."

"This one's about doing too many drugs and it's bad."

"She's saying she's fallen in love."

"He's saying he wished they'd never met."

Eva was charmed. He was roguish and handsome. And as a Finnish curator he knew everything there was to know about the art scene where she was going. He told her where to eat the best kalakukko (fish pie) and dared her to go ice-swimming. He felt real.

Or at least as real as his *Bangly* profile. What Eva didn't tell Aabel that night was that even before she met him, she knew him. He was one of the first "bangers" in London she found interesting enough to bookmark on *Bangly*, the hookup app.

It seemed as if fate had brought Aabel into her life.

She smiled to herself as she thought about the way his tight flannel shirt clung to his taut chest, and how his eyes glinted when he lamented the current art trends. Apparently, rambling was what prominent young curators from Helsinki did for a living. But Eva never got tired of listening to him. His voice alone made her wet. It sounded like a siren's song. She particularly liked how her juices clung to his mustache when he went down on her and she could taste it on his lips when he came up for a kiss.

He knew how to make a girl forget what she was running away from.

He knew the art of sexually pleasing damaged souls.

Shashi, her Wellness Guru, had recommended celibacy for her first year of sobriety, probably to protect her from situations like this. Whatever.

The smell of cologne from the bespectacled businessman sitting next to Eva drove her a little mad. It reminded her of the last night she and Aabel spent together. She remembered a bottle of Hugo Boss on his shelf. The businessman wore the same scent. It was woody and strong with a hint of citrus. She could feel her face flush with arousal.

She turned and flashed him a dirty grin.

The businessman probably thought Eva wanted to fuck him, and yeah, she did. But what she wanted most was to lean in and inhale deeply, filling her lungs with the scent.

Her burger arrived and she smiled again at the businessman. She took one large bite and let the burger juice drip around her lips as she slowly licked it up. She saw the businessman's eyes gaze at her intently. Some women didn't like to eat in front of men. In Eva's experience the most sexually satisfying ones appreciated a healthy appetite in a woman.

Tomorrow she'd be in Finland and the businessman would be home with his wife, or maybe playing golf if the weather permitted. And where the hell would Aabel be? Fucking some other brunette? She couldn't tell if he was the type, but then she didn't really know him at all, even though she must have heard his opinion on every video artist who had ever made work in Europe. All she knew was that he muttered "I really like you" once as he drifted off to sleep. And that was enough. She knew this meant he loved her. At least a little.

Do normal people feel this fucked when they fuck someone?

Is this feeling of connection even real?

The endless chattering of questions began to fill her mind. It was one of the ways Eva's addictive personality expressed itself. That, and fucking.

Are illusions worth having if they make you feel okay in the world?

Would he ever try anal?

Is sex different in Europe?

Why are men who are so good at eating pussy so bad at making coffee?

What the hell is speculative realism anyway?

Should I move to London?

What would our babies look like?

11

Eva tried to quiet her mind by focusing on remembering the first night she spent with Aabel, which was only six days ago. He had practically nothing to offer but water and a half-smoked joint. She loved that he had been in bed until the evening and his forehead dripped with sweat from a hangover. She hated sports, but loved that he wanted to watch the futbol game, and loved it even more when he talked over the entire thing. She loved that he hated people with dogs but thought people with babies were fine because they didn't impose their love on you as much. She loved when he contradicted himself while working through an idea. She loved that he fucked her when the game went into overtime and complimented her tousled hair after his team won. She loved that he didn't call when he said he would, and when she texted first she had to wait all day for a response. She loved how much that hurt.

Shashi also told her that addicts had dulled pleasure centers in their brains, and because of that the good feelings were fleeting.

When her check arrived, she signed it and then glanced coyly to her right. She caught the businessman's eye. Eva slid her spare key across the bar and then leaned over to whisper into his ear: "Room 602."

She'd seen it in the movies a million times, but was surprised it was this easy in real life.

Her heart fluttered as she walked out of the bar and made her way back to her room. She sat at the foot of the bed staring at the doorknob for what seemed forever. Chills spread over her body at the sound of the key card sliding in and the lock clicking.

"Are you a hooker or something?" he blurted out. Normally she would find that question reprehensible, but she ignored it. She was different now, after her stint at Promises. She dropped to her knees and reached for his belt buckle. He chuckled nervously, which also did not help the mood.

God, she thought, I need this.

She spotted the tan line on his finger where his wedding ring once sat and her lust intensified.

She unzipped his fly and caressed his balls. Eva had sucked enough cock to know where this was going. She wrapped her manicured fingers around his growing erection and teased him by thoroughly lubing the tip of his cock with her wide open mouth. Saliva dripped down to the base of his shaft. Then, she devoured his rigid tool, looking up at him as his cockhead touched the back of her throat. He was in a trance. His hardness pulsed at the same rate as her heartbeat, glistening from her saliva. Slowly at first, then gradually picking up the pace, Eva fucked his cock with her warm mouth. He soon started having trouble standing, so she clutched his ass with both hands to keep his dick in her mouth. Suddenly he grabbed the back of her head and began to plunge himself deeper and faster into her. Eva let out a moan of satisfaction and opened up her throat to take in every inch. Thrust after thrust she sucked him to perfection. At last he yelled, *"Scheiße!"* His whole body jerked backward as his knees buckled. Warm cum filled Eva's mouth. And she swallowed it all. She wanted to feel fucking full.

It was as if she followed an ancient dick-sucking handbook someone's older sister had passed down through the ages, one that spilled the secrets to getting your face fucked right.

After the handbook finish, Eva looked up at him. "Your turn."

Still a little dazed, he threw her onto the bed and clumsily slid her wet panties off. She pulled her dress over her head in one motion, exposing her supple and firm breasts. She'd gotten really good at that move and it never failed to impress. She slowly spread her legs to reveal her glistening wetness as he got on his knees at the foot of the bed. He then placed his hands on her calves and began to massage them firmly. Slowly, he moved his hands up her legs until they reached the sweet spot. He stared at her pussy as if he was carving a Thanksgiving turkey for the first time in front of his in-laws and didn't know where to start. He gently entered her with two fingers as he lightly rubbed her clit with his thumb. Eva's heart was pounding as she moaned and writhed on the bed. He pushed his finger deeper into her and with a gentle twist his knuckles began to rub her G-spot.

"Fuck, I'm so wet," Eva howled.

She wanted more. She grabbed his head with both hands and yanked him down between her legs. He hungrily sucked the folds of her pussy as he kept fingering her tight hole. She combed her fingers through his hair like she was stroking her pet dog as she urged him to keep pace with her building climax. He kept lapping at her wet pearl and fucking her with his fingers. Her legs began to tremble as she gasped, "Oh God, I'm close, don't stop." He pressed on, licking her clit with utter devotion.

"Right there don't stop don't stop."

"Don't stop."

"God, don't…"

Then everything around her fell into nothingness.

The best thing about married men is their years spent getting out of trouble with their wives by going down on them. You can't fake that level of experience.

On second thought, the best thing about married men is their eagerness to please.

There are few things in life that can make you feel as simultaneously high and low as fucking a man that is fucking you to avoid thinking about someone else.

III

BREAK WITH THE PAST BUT DON'T SHUT IT OUT

Eva knew how to avoid things. She was very good at it. A goddamn black belt ninja master of avoidance. Whenever she wanted to distract herself from how she was really feeling, she conjured up endless numbers of questions in her mind. And when she wanted to avoid dealing with her well-being (or lack thereof), Eva always found ways to keep herself busy, which usually involved getting so aroused she couldn't see straight. It was easier that way.

Besides, Eva was tired of talking about the mess that was her life. People hit bottom for any number of reasons. Insurmountable debt from getting a student loan to study Japanese conceptual art of the 1960s, for example. Or looking for love in deeply damaging relationships, like the kind where he says he wants to cum inside you so you can carry his seed and be with him forever and you scream back that you don't even love him anymore and are irritated by his every move then he kicks you out of his apartment at four in the morning and you sit outside his door sobbing because you are too drunk to drive home.

The truth was that she felt embarrassed talking about her mess. Her lowest point—

the bottom—felt like such a cliché; debilitating depression that led to erratic and self-destructive acts, like snorting coke off her gallery dealer's cock. It wasn't even a special occasion. It was a Tuesday.

Afternoon.

Eva had found a great deal of success right out of grad school, a feat that was rare for young artists, especially women. Her work rested comfortably between technology, narcissism, and snark in a way that seemed to resonate with her generation. She made room size installations and video pieces that first caught the attention of other artists, and then critics and dealers. The buzz around her career usually involved the word luck, but the truth was that Eva worked her ass off day in and day out with little to no sleep and financed all the projects on her own.

At first the exhibition openings and parties were merely a formality and a nice break from working so hard in the studio. But as her star rose, the parties began to eclipse her practice and she pursued them with as much passion as she put into her work. Eva's quick ascendance gave her what she thought she wanted: excitement and attention.

The critics loved her. Other artists began talking shit about her, which Eva liked because she figured you're nobody unless someone is hating on you. She felt at home with all the glamour and gossip.

But it took a toll. Despite her achievements, she was still tending to a six figure student loan debt. And the more she worked, the less the work seemed to matter. She lost whatever grounding she had in making art and couldn't bear the thought of being in the studio, alone. A sense of resentment slowly crept into her mind.

They say it's not truly the bottom if you don't lose it all. And it's not like she drove her car off the road or woke up on the subway without shoes. But she fell, hard. What does the bottom feel like? For Eva it was a foggy feeling from deep in her gut that made it impossible to sleep. It was like a Xanax haze but without any of the benefits. She became increasingly withdrawn, from herself and everybody around her. After a while she couldn't even muster the energy or will to take in full breaths. She was drowning in her own discontent. And that's when she thought about withdrawing from the world on a permanent basis.

How much better would I feel if I were dead?
Would the prices of my artwork rise?

Who would mount the retrospective? MoMA? Pompidou?

What is fucking like in the afterlife?

If you're horny in the afterlife, do you still get wet—even though you don't have a body?

Eva knew she needed help. She checked herself into Promises, a vaguely religious rehab center in upstate New York. It was a six-week twelve-step program tucked into the backwoods of the Adirondacks. The closest bar was about 50 miles away (she checked on Google Maps before they confiscated her phone). For weeks Eva followed a daily routine guided by the "twelve promises." Every morning she emerged from her dormitory and joined other rehabbers on the lawn to recite them out loud before heading to the morning yoga sessions. She tried to suppress her dirty thoughts as she stretched her fingertips to the sky, and then did the Downward Dog. She dutifully ate the monastically inspired "Merry Martyr" cuisine they served for breakfast, lunch, and dinner. She even resisted the urge to buy weed from the sweet fat guy who probably smuggled it in by sticking it in his rectum. Shashi, her pathologically calm "Wellness Guru," looked so pleased with her that she even shed a few tears when Eva talked about her childhood in a Promises-based group session.

Eva found the "promises" as inspiring as the wisdom from fortune cookies. But over time, between the recitations, the exercises, and all the free range barley gruel anyone would ever want to eat, Eva began to breathe a little more easily. And after only three weeks she found her way back from deep depression to merely being anxious and unhappy.

She felt normal again.

So much so that she decided to bail out of the program. Eva needed to escape from her newfound sense of well-being. Luckily, she hadn't burned all of her bridges on the way down and still had a few favors to cash in overseas. A friend of a friend of a performance artist she used to fuck pulled some strings with an artist residency in the Finnish countryside, where Eva could go for a few weeks in an attempt to get her work and life going again, on her own terms. But first, before she got herself back on track, she wanted to see her friend Fawn, in London, and get into some trouble. And that's where she met Aabel, and found herself better, and worse, than before.

IV

TOUCH OTHERS LIKE YOU WANT TO BE TOUCHED

Eva hopped in a cab in front of her hotel and headed to Heathrow. After a week in London she was ready to leave. She checked her phone. No texts. She had not heard from Aabel for two days.

Three cramped hours later she stepped onto the tarmac of the tiny Finnish airport. The sun was peaking just above some ridiculously picturesque mountains beyond the runway. She breathed in the crisp country air, hard, so she could really feel it. She couldn't believe how fresh and rejuvenating it felt. After being slowly poisoned by the air she was breathing back across the Atlantic, Eva needed this. She wondered how much oxygen it would take to shake her out of the stupor that was her New York state of mind.

A curiously bubbly intern from the residency retrieved her from the airport and they stopped by a local market on the way there. The hubris of traveling to a foreign country having made no attempt to learn even a bit of the native language smacked her in the face as she bumbled through the store trying to purchase some basics. Which coffee is the one that doesn't suck, and is this yogurt, or sour cream, or crème fraîche? Her credit card didn't work at the register and she stared blankly at the cashier until he snatched it from her hand, finishing the transaction on his own.

Is this why people hate Americans?

Why am I so ridiculous?

Are Finnish condoms different?

Some kind of rare animal skin?

Baby seal?

Reindeer?

Is there such a thing as a reindeer dildo?

The residency was located in a small farming town outside of Espoo, Finland's second largest city—which really wasn't saying much. As she decamped from the car reserved for residency use, she found herself surrounded by green and sunshine and spongy moss that made everything sort of look like a fairy tale. Eva was thoroughly enchanted.

The residency buildings consisted of a solidly built lodge, a barn repurposed as a studio and workshop, a tech center, and a sauna. Everything exuded a peculiar mix of Middle Earth and modernist, as if Hobbits had designed for Ikea. It was a nice change of pace from the ascetic vibe of Jesus rehab camp.

At first glance Eva didn't find any of her fellow artists-in-residence particularly attractive. But unlike the rehabbers, her new companions exuded a certain confidence and ambition. They gave her something she had not felt in quite some time: hope. Eva even began to feel that if she spent a few weeks here doing nothing but plan her next project, she would be ready to kick her career back into gear.

She settled in quickly. Eva sat outside alone almost everyday, drawing and writing, a bit away from the house, but not too far. And almost every day she could hear, but not see, Jussi working outside.

One day she heard some sort of drill, or maybe a sander.

The next day he was using a saw. Or a loud and whiny donkey.

Jussi was the director of the residency. He was thirty-something, tall, and rugged. He looked like he could wield an ax and most likely build a fire. Eva and Jussi had corresponded frequently before her trip, mostly about travel schedules and accommodations. Everything was strictly professional until Eva met him in person. It was then that she realized just how sexy he was. She quickly went back and reread all the emails, looking for signs that he was flirting with her.

Her limited knowledge of saunas

didn't help matters, Eva thought. She knew they existed and that Finland was famous for them. But she wasn't sure how they worked or how you were supposed to seduce somebody in one. She knew there was one on site and that hot rocks and nudity were involved.

Does steam hurt or help the libido?

Is sauna a Finnish word for steam sex?

Does cum taste the same if it's heated?

When a rock is hot, is it heavier?

Instead of a rock, can it be something soft, like cheese?

Is there incense?

Rose petals?

Is it possible to be too hot to have sex?

Is sexual tension different in Europe?

Seeing Jussi in person was no disappointment. In fact, he was even more handsome because he was constantly doing repairs. In New York she was accustomed to men adept at little other than snarky quips. The sound of Jussi's drill was enough to get her going. She liked listening to him work. She liked that he knew *how* to work.

On the days he worked inside, she sat on the lawn right in front of his office and remained ever present, on the off chance he'd happen to glance out of his window. Sheer persistence had worked in her favor in the past, and she firmly believed that projecting sexual energy in his general vicinity could prove fruitful.

Eva learned most of her moves from *Lolita*, the book and one of the movies. There was the one where you hold a glance for an extraordinary length of time. Or smile innocently, averting your eyes quickly when contact is made. She also got a few tips from *Gossip Girl*, like standing with your back to him, twirling your hair slightly upwards to expose the nape of the neck. Sometimes she could pull off those moves in the vein of a sexy young vixen. But mostly they tended to feel like the awkward tics of a teenager with autism.

Somehow Jussi managed to skillfully deflect all of her advances without overtly turning her down, and she couldn't tell if he was being professional or just flat out uninterested. But Eva didn't care. Once she set her mind on a dick, there was no going back.

One of the assistants let it slip that Jussi liked to collect various old things, like broken vintage stoves or knives with deer hooves as handles, and would speak about them excitedly at length if given the opportunity. At least collections were less offensive than sports statistics or obscure band discographies, but let's be honest, only by a little. She resigned herself to the reality that as a straight woman she was likely to grow old and die next to someone who chatters on endlessly about mostly unimportant and uninteresting details. And that was if she was lucky.

Eva poked her head into Jussi's office the next morning She plopped herself down at the end of the desk wearing a pair of short shorts and started to ask him questions about the old trash in her workshop area—could some of it potentially be viewed as valuable? Jussi glanced up from his office chair, eyeing her long, bare legs like the hat-wearing villain in a *film noir*.

How long can I maintain a sexy pose?

Am I losing feeling in my legs?

How long do I have to wait until I get a clear sign from him?

If there is no clear signal, can I can sneak into his room at night and slide his hard cock into me without seeming like I'm crazy?

Am I crazy or just horny?

Is there a difference?

What would it feel like with him deep inside me, his hands wrapped around my neck?

Or him grabbing his manhood and gagging my throat with it?

Jussi just smiled and continued to fill out paperwork. That was it. Nothing. She had to get out of there. Out of this residency and this prison cell of hormonal torture.

Eva walked out of the office. She reached into her back pocket and took out her phone. She tapped on the icon for

Bangly in search of local men to satisfy her.

She logged in and waited for the results. Candidates began to appear on the screen.

Onni, 45, soul patches. Missing left eye.

Juho, 26, gelled back hair. Loves gangbangs.

Toivo, 39, tribal tattoos.

LOL.

She expanded her parameters, mile by mile, until she found Einar, an acceptably handsome man living in Helsinki.

Eva went back to her room and locked the door. She opened her laptop and booked a bus ticket for Helsinki the next day.

She had packed her trusty pocket-rocket vibrator and was ready for some release. But in the cruel cosmic joke that had become her life, she hadn't packed any batteries. She threw the silver vibrator across the room. Then she closed her eyes and slid her panties to the side. With her middle finger and forefinger she explored her wetness, lightly at first, applying more pressure the farther south her fingers traveled. She closed her eyes and imagined a perfect specimen of a man kneeling behind her, fingering her slit and telling her all the filthy things he was going to do to her. She perched on her knees and stuck her ass in the air as she moaned softly, spreading her legs as wide as they could go.

Her imaginary lover then got on his back and slid his head between her legs. His tongue picked up where his fingers left off, sucking her wet flesh. Her juices covered her fingers as she drove them deeper into her hot hole, struggling to keep pace with the impossibly nubile tongue pleasuring her in her imagination.

Jussi faded from her memory as she writhed and moaned on the floor with Einar on her mind.

V

FIND THE STRENGTH TO *KNOW* YOURSELF

guess 3 things bout me fr
my pics then ill do urs :-)

When her host, Inga, took her around Helsinki she felt like she was sixteen again and in her parents' living room at their annual Christmas party. Inga was as tall and as strikingly blonde as a drag queen. She was also manically friendly.

They could barely go anywhere without having to stop and chat. She even struck up a conversation with the local police on the street, which Eva found unnerving. Who talks to cops, unless you're trying to talk them out of beating the shit out of you? Besides, Eva's social existence relied heavily on opportunities to disappear into crowds, unless she was drunk. So the happy vibe (and the fact she was sober) was dampening her spirits, to say the least. But to be fair, people were friendly. And it was summer. Though, as far as Eva could tell, summer in Finland was winter everywhere else.

u still there?

Inga knew every guy in the five-mile radius that appeared on Eva's *Bangly* screen. "Cool cool he works at the fancy clothing shop." "Wow that's my boyfriend's cousin wow cool." "This guy is gay yeah cool super cool." "Oh Einar fun super cool too you should go out with him yeah cool."

That was enough for Eva. She replied to Einar on her phone. When she hit the Send button she felt relieved. Eva had been praying every morning for peace of mind but still felt she was slipping back into her old habits. Questions popped into her mind out of nowhere and she couldn't control them. She desperately needed to get out of her thoughts and into someone's bed.

tell me a secret cutie

im afraid of heights

eh…

i fucked during overtime when World Cup soccer game ws on

who was playing? u want to come over n watch a movie?

Two hours later, Eva stood in front of a set of glass doors. They flung open and there was Einar, 31. Dark brown hair. Hazel eyes. Large hands. He didn't look like his pictures but … whatever. She followed him into his spacious and oddly clean apartment. No empty beer bottles anywhere. No clothes on the floor. There was nothing on the marble countertop in his kitchenette except a white orchid in a slender glass vase. Did this guy clean his apartment for her, or was it always this neat?

Eva tried to remember how tidy the apartment was in *American Psycho*.

They sat down on his couch, spent what seemed like too long a time discussing movies. It wasn't bad except for the sinister little grins and chuckles he kept throwing her way as he described films they could watch.

This one is on whale hunting and is sad (smirk).

This one is an action-packed conspiracy and has murder (sinister laugh).

They settled on *Funny Games*, by Michael Haneke. Einar grabbed his laptop and pointed in the general direction of his bedroom.

"Let's watch it in there," he said matter-of-factly.

She liked how assertive he was. She

had read about the hookup culture in Finland. And apparently it was normal for people to stumble into each other's beds after the pubs closed, whether they were drunk or not. And here she was, doing her best to fit in.

They walked into his bedroom. He set his laptop on the bedside table and got under the blue satin sheets.

"You aren't even going to pretend to watch the movie, huh?" she asked.

"This just feels right."

He leaned in for a kiss.

It struck her in that very moment that her life had become one of those romantic comedies no one watches and everyone hates. Eva let out a laugh before Einar's lips landed on hers. He playfully bit at her lower lip and then slipped his tongue into her mouth.

To Eva's surprise, Einar was right. It did feel right.

She kissed him back harder and wetter, as if she was daring him.

Einar's hand strayed to cup one of her firm breasts, massaging her hardening nipple with his thumb and forefinger. Eva squirmed with every touch as she plunged her tongue deeper into his mouth. Einar unbuttoned her blouse, revealing her supple body. He brushed his fingers lightly along her neck and shoulders and down toward her hips, sending chills down her spine. He leaned down and kissed her firm mounds, softly at first, caressing them with his lips, and then more boldly by playfully biting her nipples. Eva arched her back and ran her fingers through Einar's hair. She breathed deeply as she marveled at how he looked as perfectly groomed as the young men in the Haneke film that played in the background.

Einar snaked his hand down the back of her jeans and teasingly pulled at her black thong. Eva could feel her thong straining against her aching pussy. She was soaking wet.

He stood up in the middle of the bed, towering over her body. He quickly shed his pants and his growing shaft rose out of his white boxers. He bent over, grabbed her hips, and ripped her jeans off like a man possessed. The little sinister laugh returned as he looked at her lying on the bed with her nipples hard and pussy wet. He ran his powerful hands against her flesh and pulled her thong off.

Einar got down on his knees and spread Eva's legs. He tilted forward and opened the lips of her wetness part, and then drove his forefinger inside her. Eva gasped as he worked her with his fingers in a slow and steady rhythm. Every stroke pushed her closer to the edge. He lowered his head and began to lick, flicking his tongue back and forth over pussy folds. Eva grabbed his head and took control of how she wanted to be pleased, guiding him up and down her velvet patch.

"Right there right there," Eva groaned.

Einar found the spot and he encircled it with his tongue as his hands firmly caressed her upper body. He could feel Eva's muscles in her hole clench and it drove him wild. He pushed his tongue deep into her and Eva purred approvingly. Einar quickened his pace.

"Keep going, don't stop don't stop."

Her legs locked around Einar's head. Her face and chest turned red as she rocked to and fro on the bed. She arched her back and pushed her cunt hard into Einar's face to savor every last lick. Waves of the orgasm washed over her body as she felt completely enveloped by sweet pleasure.

"Einar, 31" seemed to know what the fuck he was doing.

Still recovering from her dreamy, post-come state, she winked at Einar and signaled him to lie next to her on the bed. She then got on her knees and began to stroke his hard cock with one hand. With the other hand she gingerly ran her fingers over his entire body, tickling every crevice and fold. Einar shivered and smiled, lying in wait for what would come next. She then straddled him and massaged her aching clit with just the tip of his manhood. She laughed as she teased him by hovering her cunt over his cockhead and letting it slide into her a bit, only to raise her hips the next second and let it slip out.

Einar reached toward the bedside table and grabbed a condom. Eva saw it in his hand and felt relieved. Safe sex was the only thing left that made her feel less insane and more in control. But as he ripped the foil and put the rubber over his cock, Eva's mind began to spin.

Rubber?

Bearskin?

Shark cartilage?

Organic hemp?

Tibetan silk collected by horny monks?

Einar quickly rolled on the condom, placed his hands on Eva's hips and lowered her onto his rigid cock until she sat at its base. Eva let out a muffled yell as he filled her tight hole completely. Einar fondled Eva's firm breasts as she began to ride him in earnest, rocking her hips back and forth with greater and greater speed. Suddenly, in one fluid motion, he flipped her over while remaining inside her. He spread her legs wide and held onto her ankles as he plunged into her with a fury. Eva moaned in delight as she humped her pelvis forward to meet his every thrust. She stretched her arms out wide and grabbed onto the sides of the bed, bracing herself against Einar. He looked into Eva's eyes as she was staring into his. And she was surprised to find how in the midst of this epic fuck his face remained calm, almost serene.

It went on for what seemed like hours. He was the type Eva thought existed only in the fictional exploits of heroes like Thor, if Thor starred in pornos like *Meathammers 3*.

Thunder rumbled overhead as Thor rode Eva. She could feel another epic storm brewing. She thrashed her head from side to side as Einar continued to pound her mercilessly. He spread her legs as wide as they could go, and then began to rub her clit with his right hand as he fucked her.

"Come on, give it to me," Eva egged him on. "Harder."

Her voice sent spasms up and down Einar's body. He could no longer hold it back and erupted like a glorious Finnish geyser.

Completely spent, Einar fell into an exhausted heap next to Eva. He turned his head and she could see a satisfied grin spread across his face. Against all her instincts, she smiled back.

"So—Eva, right?"

VI

THRIVE IN THE UNKNOWN

Einar closed his eyes and drifted off to sleep. Typical, right? Eva never understood how anyone could fall asleep after coming. She was so alert she wanted to paint four gigantic paintings inspired by Einar's dick, or lift a car, or something. For Eva, orgasms rejuvenated the senses. They shook her out of the stupor of her waking life. It had been that way since she was a preteen, when she first learned to touch herself while trying on leggings in the changing room of Wet Seal at the mall.

It was also profoundly reassuring for Eva to have such an intense orgasm with someone she cared so little about.

She got out of bed and reached for her jeans. She grabbed her phone from the back pocket and tapped the screen. No messages.

Where is he?

Why hasn't he texted?

Does he really think Doug Aitken is an overrated douche?

Where is *he?*

She tried to get out of her own head. She sat next to the bedside table and opened Einar's laptop. She found a copy of *Taken 3* on his desktop and double-clicked the file. Eva had always loved Liam Neeson and it warmed her heart knowing his work had only become better since *Schindler's List*. She crawled back into bed and laid her head on Einar's shoulder. She found one of his hands and intertwined her fingers with his. Holding Einar's hand brought Eva back to reality. It was an intimate gesture for two people who barely knew each other. But Eva found it comforting. It was nice to hold and be held, even if the other person was unconscious.

Was Aabel thinking of her?

At the moment it didn't matter.

Sometimes you fall for a man just enough to enjoy his company. You put up with him babbling about *Gutai* or hedge funds, or whatever, because after he is done talking he spreads your legs and goes down on you long and hard, like he's swimming the butterfly stroke at the Olympics. But if he asked you to get serious you'd say you have to think about it, putting off the answer as long as possible, which typically means until he moves on. Eva was familiar with these kinds of men. How fucked up and fun they can be and how screwed up they are in reality.

They were the only ones Eva ever paid any attention to and wanted. But the truth was that they weren't even really men. They were more like different models of smart phones from the same brand that Eva had gotten used to buying. They were good enough until they weren't. And that was when she would get the next upgrade.

The battery on the laptop ran out of juice and the screen went black. There was an eerie silence in the room. Eva looked at Einar. Still asleep. She untangled her hand from his and lightly petted his disheveled hair. She picked up her clothes and tiptoed out of the bedroom, got dressed, and left.

VII

CONFRONT THE FEARS THAT DEFINE YOU

A few hours later the bus pulled into that dinky Finnish town she had escaped from just days ago. She hailed a taxi at the bus station to take her back to the residency. When she arrived she saw someone standing next to the front gates of the compound.

It was Jussi.

"Nice to see you," he said.

"Nice to see you too," Eva replied with

a mischievous grin.

"I've missed you," he said, with the same damn grin.

Eva's mind would typically start to fill with questions in a situation like this, so she would be too distracted to actually feel and try to understand what was happening. But this time was different. Eva had only one question in mind.

If you put positive energy into the world, do you get a throbbing cock in return?

Eva felt renewed after being with Einar and thought that her sexual mojo was back, although she never imagined the sexy sit-on-the-desk move would work so fast. During her brief heyday as one of the New York artists to watch under thirty she blew through hot muses like a white, male painter. But since rehab, she'd had to sing harder for her supper. She wasn't used to working so much for a man, and Jussi was making her work for it. Or at least she thought he was.

"Need to freshen up. Had a long night of great sex and an even longer bus ride after," Eva said.

She walked on and left him standing there.

A couple of steps later she turned around.

"I think my shower's broken. Think you can give me a hand?" she asked.

Jussi smiled and followed her. It was early, so no one was out. A light fog blanketed the area. Out of the blue, he grabbed her from behind and kissed the back of her neck. Eva was startled at first, but she could also feel herself becoming aroused. Her nipples instantly became erect and poked against her t-shirt.

Jussi leaned into Eva's back and grabbed her hips. She could feel his warm breath on her neck, and it turned her on. Eva let out a whimper as he slid one hand down the front of her tight pants. Starting in a slow, circular fashion, his fingers stroked her cunt underneath her damp black thong. Then he began to alternate his rhythm, rubbing faster or slower as she started to grind her firm ass against his pelvis and moan with greater and greater abandon. She didn't care who heard her at this point. She closed her eyes. She wanted him. She wanted every inch of him inside her.

But not just yet.

Because in spite of her exhibitionist streak, Eva felt a little vulnerable being groped by Jussi in the middle of a courtyard. Her door was only twenty steps away. Eva came to her senses and yanked Jussi's hand out of her pants and made a run for it, looking back at Jussi and flashing a wicked grin. When she reached the door she took out her key and shoved it into the doorknob. But the door wouldn't open, and while she fumbled with the lock Jussi came up behind her and lightly caressed her backside in a way that was more ticklish than arousing. Surprised, she jumped back and dropped the keys.

Jussi chuckled.

Eva laughed too.

He picked up the key and opened the door. Once inside, Eva inadvertently knocked over the little glass jar with the pinecones that the staff had left on the bedside table for local charm. "I'm so sorry!" Eva squealed at a pitch slightly above awkward. She walked toward Jussi to kiss him but she stepped on the jar and she slipped, lunging toward him instead.

Foreheads collided with a loud bang and they collapsed onto the floor, both holding their heads.

Jussi was splayed on the floor with Eva next to him. She reached out to touch his shoulder to see if he was okay. He nodded, but looked a little dazed.

Desperation began to set in.

Maybe the moment has passed?

But isn't there always a moment?

Isn't this another moment?

Right now?

Or now?

Who's to say this moment is any better or worse than that moment?

Can't you shut the fuck up, Eva?

Maybe she could ride him like a bike— a very tall, ruggedly handsome bike with a bit of a language barrier.

She took in a deep breath and managed to crawl on top of Jussi. She gave him a luscious kiss on the mouth and pressed her hands into his muscular torso, acting as if she was giving him a dirty version of CPR. Jussi started to come back to life. He slipped his hands under Eva's t-shirt and artfully toyed with her swollen nipples. Eva kissed him even more deeply, holding the sides of his face and plunging her tongue down his throat. She was ready. Eva scooted down and unbuttoned Jussi's pants and out popped his long and throbbing rod. She opened her mouth as wide as it would go and swallowed his cock whole, closing her lips around it and swirling around it with her tongue, feeling it rock back and forth inside her. The sensation of his swelling shaft thrilled her. Jussi lifted his hips off the floor to get a better angle and she took him deeper into her throat.

Eva slipped one hand between her legs and played with herself. She began by curling her fingers and rubbing her wet slit at a slow and steady pace, but gradually built up momentum. She stroked herself faster and faster until she couldn't take it anymore, and then pumped her fingers deep into her waiting cunt as she took Jussi's rod out of her mouth and teasingly licked the head. Jussi muttered something in Finnish, which Eva assumed meant he approved of her technique. As she worked him with her lips and tongue, his hips began to thrust in rhythm and his breathing deepened. She reached down and played with his balls, and Jussi moaned even louder.

Pulling her mouth away from his cock, Eva looked up to make eye contact. "Cum for me, my exotic Finnish stallion," she purred in an ironic yet lusty voice while she jerked his wet and sticky shaft off.

That did it. Jussi let out a deep, hoarse grunt as his man-milk shot wildly and everywhere. She rubbed the remaining dribble onto his still semi-hard cock, which made him moan and twitch on the floor. Her hand, arm, and breasts were covered in his juice.

Eva sat back and smiled, taking pride in her handiwork.

Jussi suddenly rolled Eva over on her stomach and got on top of her. He gripped both her hands and pushed them above her head, pinning her to the floor. Eva squirmed and struggled underneath his body as he straddled her.

"You want this cock, don't you?"

"Yes, please, give it to me," Eva whimpered.

He let go of her arms and wrapped his

rough and calloused hands around her throat. She could feel his determination to use her like a fuck doll.

"Do you think you deserve it?" he hissed.

Eva could feel his tool hardening again. She arched her back and pushed her ass against him.

"What do I have to do to deserve it?" she mockingly pleaded.

He leaned down and licked her earlobe, then kissed her on the side of her mouth. He then snaked one hand between her thighs. Her whole body stiffened with anticipation. She then felt something cold, something hard, against her ass. Eva was usually not into toys, but right now she craved something raw and savage.

She turned her head and looked down as Jussi slowly inserted the giant metallic dildo into her tight hole.

"Oh God," Eva squealed. She couldn't believe how big it felt. Her muscles began to flex and ripple to accommodate the metal rod thrusting into her. She found herself getting wetter still, and gradually the discomfort faded, replaced by an overwhelming sense of fullness. With his other hand Jussi began to massage her clit with enough pressure to keep her wanting more but not enough to make her come.

Eva felt like her entire body was vibrating. And with each stroke of the dildo her arousal was amplified. Her legs tightened, her back arched, and her ass pushed upwards, spurring him on.

He drew his hand and slapped Eva's rosy cheeks hard. He repeated this several times before she started to cry out.

"Now I want you to come for me," he growled, and with a single thrust he plunged his shaft straight into her slit, burying it all the way to the base. Her arousal intensified with each penetration as Eva gasped for breath, trying to take it all in.

Yes?

"Yes!"

More?

"More!"

She could no longer hold back. She made a deep animal noise as she came, and an overwhelming sensation tore through her body.

VIII

TAKE THE TIME TO ENJOY BEING *HERE*

IX

CHANGE YOUR OUTLOOK AND THE REST WILL FOLLOW

Someone with a cruel sense of humor once said an artist who doesn't want to teach is like a woman who doesn't want to have kids. Eva never wanted to teach. But her situation didn't leave her many options.

She didn't want to stay at the residency and she didn't want to go back to New York either. Luckily, an arts academy in Munich invited her as a visiting artist for the summer, and while she loathed the idea, it gave her an excuse to leave yet again. She still hadn't heard a word from Aabel, even though she drafted what seemed like hundreds of sexts and sad texts to him, detailing every one of her clingy, horny feelings. Of course she never sent them. It's supposed to be therapeutic, said the Internet.

She emailed the academy and accepted the position, having convinced herself that a hot young German student would take her mind off things.

Why not add "pedagogical predator" to her growing list of prospective careers?

On her first day Eva looked hot. Her white blouse was tight enough to hint at her sexy black bra underneath. She could feel the students staring at her, and at first she almost didn't know what to do.

They were barely younger than she, so she couldn't really fantasize about being a cougar on the prowl for innocent prey. In their eyes she could be the "cool teacher," someone they could grab a drink with after class, or perhaps even befriend if they had met under different circumstances.

Eva eyed the older teachers with envy, especially the brooding curatorial professor, Frederik. He had a tall, solid frame with a bit of a belly, and a salt-and-peppery receding hairline.

Students flocked to him, hanging on his every word. It's funny how desire can be contagious, as if people just want what others want because it feels good to want the same thing.

Eva found herself lingering a bit too long in the teachers' lounge when he poured his morning coffee. Sometimes she wanted his attention bad enough that she would pass by him seductively, making sure she moved her hips close enough to rub her ass up against him in her tight black pencil skirt. One time Eva swore she felt him get hard.

Frederik's position as a well-respected contemporary curator at a major Austrian museum added another dimension to her growing interest. He was a curator. She was an artist. It didn't take much imagination to envision what effect he would have on her career if her mouth found its way around his cock.

Eva had been struggling to make new work since she left rehab and was beginning to fear that she wouldn't be able to do so again without her vices. Sleeping her way to an exhibition wasn't ideal, but the thought of showing again gave her a glimmer of hope. And everyone knows hope is a form of addiction.

One morning Frederik stayed a little longer in the lounge, smiling politely at the other teachers. This was unusual, as every other day he would pour his coffee and look over his notes while grumbling, being careful to avoid eye contact with virtually everyone. "Ahem," came a clearing of the throat by Frederik. "I just wanted to let you all know that my class will be traveling to Vienna this weekend for a special guided tour of my museum. You are welcome to join us if you'd like." Frederik looked over coldly at Eva, then at her breasts, then down to her long, dark red fingernails.

Eva's class joined in on the trip to the museum, and Frederik doled out affection to his students while completely ignoring

her. The art world was overrun with curmudgeonly daddies, but at the academy
Frederik was the big fish and he knew it.
Eva grew impatient and decided to sneak
out of the group tour, leaving her students
to drool over Professor Prude.

On her way out of the museum she
undid the strap under her blouse and re-
moved her bra swiftly under her sleeve
like the professional she was. She casu-
ally tucked it into her bag on top of her
textbooks. She spit into her cleavage and
started to massage her tits to give them a
little shine. She didn't feel like the same
desperate ball of anxiety that first stepped
off that plane in Finland. She was in thigh-
high stockings, running down the streets
of Vienna. She had a hookup app and a
growing sense of her own self worth. She
took her phone out of her bag and tapped
on the icon for *Bangly*.

X

IMAGINE A FULLER FUNDAMENT

Eva loved contemporary conceptual art, and so did the Austrians. This was why being in Vienna was such a perfect match. All of her carefully crafted pretensions were catered to in the tastefully sparse galleries. She practically floated from kunsthalle to kunsthalle, each one more visually severe and spartan than the last.

The last museum she visited that day

seemed at first glance to be completely bare, with nothing but clean white walls. The artist had separated the gallery into small rooms. A single white vitrine was installed in the middle of each room. Most of the vitrines contained a single white piece of paper with only a few words written on it. They listed in German everything the artist did for a month— everything he ate, drank, smoked, read, and saw wherever he went. Some of the papers were intentionally left blank without any explanation. Some vitrines contained nothing at all.

Her heart soared. She felt at home.

Then her phone buzzed. It was *Bangly*.

> You have a new message from:
> Hols, 26.

do u live in wien eva?

no just here 4 visit i live in NYC

oh i love NYC ill have to visit u someday :)

do u live near the museum quartier hols

i do

wud u like 2 get a drink

or maybe a ONS

whats ONS

one nite stand

u might have 2 tell me a little bit abt urself 1st

what do u want 2 know

how big n how hard is ur cock

only if u tell me how tight n wet is ur pussy

meet at museum in 10 min 3rd floor cum find me ;)

Eva could feel herself getting aroused at the thought of Hols seeking her out in the art space. Vienna was quiet in the summer and the museum was almost deserted. She scoped out a proper place

90

to fuck a complete stranger. The rooms where video works were installed looked promising. They were secluded, dark, and soundproofed. But she obviously wasn't the only one who'd noticed their potential for debauchery; a security guard popped in every five to ten minutes. Eva was headed to the restroom in search of a more appropriate locale when she felt a tap on her shoulder.

"Eva?"

Before she even had the chance to consider regret, there he stood, in front of the restroom door. She was face to face with Hols, 26. Eva was pleasantly surprised. Having barely looked at his profile before inviting him to meet, her mental picture had been a little fuzzy. But it seemed that someone above was on her side. Without speaking a word they barreled together through the restroom door.

It was more like a rest-closet. They stood with their bodies touching, his hot breath on her neck. Their lips met and their tongues darted back and forth in each other's mouths. She could feel his massive hard-on protruding from his jeans and caressed it with one hand.

Hols broke their kiss and beamed at her with a devilish twinkle in his eye. He bit his lip and grabbed her by the shoulders, spinning her around. She pushed herself against his chest and he pressed his swelling shaft into the small of her back. She heard the jingle of his belt buckle unfastening and felt him nibble lightly at the delicate spot where her neck and shoulders meet. He clutched her thighs before pulling her short black skirt upwards. His bare skin pressed against hers as he pinched her thong with his fingers and pulled it to one side, exposing her moist muff. Eva felt shivers down her spine as Hols dropped to his knees. He slowly ran the tip of his tongue from her asshole to her clit, lingering there as her legs shook. She could feel her juices dripping down her thighs.

She placed her palms against the cold white tiles on the wall and stuck her ass out even more as Hols ate her from behind. Eva couldn't get enough of it and began to grind her tail into his face, savoring each rough lick. He plunged his tongue into her tight rim and fingered her cunt at the same time, driving Eva wild.

He then stood up and gently nudged the tip of his shaft into her wet slit. Hols was much taller than Eva, so she had to stand on her toes for him to properly fuck her. He grabbed her by the hips and slowly entered her. She let out a quiet yelp as he pushed deeper into her hot hole. His cock began to slam her hard, pinning Eva to the wall, so that her toes were barely touching the floor. She could feel every vein and curve on his massive rod as he pounded her tight hole from behind. His fingernails dug almost painfully into her hips and his roughness filled her with joy as her pussy tightened around his glorious tool.

All of a sudden, the door flew open. In the heat of the moment neither one had thought to lock it behind them.

There stood Frederik, a stunned look on his curmudgeonly face.

Eva wasn't sure at first if he had recognized her, but when their eyes met it was clear Frederik knew exactly what was going on.

Hols didn't even seem to notice the intruder. He kept pumping away furiously while Frederik stood there, mouth agape and eyes bulging.

Oh God, my job! was Eva's first reaction. But then she came to her senses.

Oh fuck it!

Keep fucking me.

Fuck me.

Just like this.

Don't stop.

Don't stop!

She flashed a look-at-what-you've-been-missing wink at Frederik, and slammed the door in his face. She lifted her left leg and rammed her foot up on the toilet seat for better leverage. Hols wrapped his arms around her rib cage for more control.

If sex was a drug, Eva was definitely peaking.

Hols grabbed her hair around his fist and pulled hard enough to snap her head back, making her nipples rub hard against her blouse. With her back arched he drove into Eva even more deeply. She reached down with one hand and stroked her swollen clit over and over again and her whole body began to twitch with anticipation. She could feel herself starting to climax.

Eva then heard the long, drawn-out creak of the door being eased open again. Eva turned her head and saw Frederik standing there, as if he'd never left. Without warning he squeezed himself into the stall with the lovers, his flabby tummy brushing against them as he crept by and closed the door behind him. Eva was shocked but her mind was concentrating on milking the most out of Hols's savage pounding.

Frederik pinched Eva's nipple to test the waters. She didn't know whether to scream or just go with it. So she did both. She let out a loud moan as she looked at Frederik, managing a half smile. He then reached between her legs and began to finger her slick pearl. Frederik started to sweat as he unfastened his pants and began to stroke himself, predictably mumbling something about a solo show in Eva's future. Hols pulled out and let Frederik step behind her. She bent forward to take Hols in her mouth while Frederik slid inside.

If it was possible to black out on dick, Eva was about to lose it.

Her phone buzzed again as she started to come.

> You have a new message from: Aabel, 33.

XI

CREATE THE SERENITY FROM WITHIN

hey

When is the next flight to London?

Could I get on it?

Should I even go?

What the hell has he been doing this whole time?

Is he fucking Fawn?

Was it only three weeks ago?

Did he add the extra "a" in his name just to mess with people?

How does he do that with only one tongue?

Does he miss me?

How bad does he miss me if he misses me?

If he doesn't miss me, is it wrong for me to hope that he contracts Ebola?

Or Chlamydia?

Or Lyme disease?

Is Lyme disease just an American thing?

Am I just an easy American fuck to him?

Why do I love to fuck him?

Why do I care if he misses me?

Does he care about futbol more than Harun Farocki?

Does he care about me more than Harun Farocki?

That's not fair, I know, how about, does he love me more than Ragnar Kjartansson?

Pipilotti Rist?

Group Material?

Yvonne Rainer?

At least more than Douglas Gordon, right?

> sry ive been out of touch u
> still in helsnki

Has he been checking up on me on **Bangly**?

Does he know about Einar?

Jussi?

What if he's related to Jussi?

What if they are brothers?

If I fucked two brothers, do they know somehow through telepathy or some shit?

Is this some sick game between two brothers to fuck the same girl?

Is it still a sick game if it turns the girl on?

Would I fuck them at the same time?

Would they fuck each other afterwards?

Would I be jealous?

Is jealousy a turn on or turn off?

Does he think about me when he masturbates?

Does he see me or my ass?

Does he imagine me on all fours or on my back?

if ur back in London wud luv 2 c u

XII

MASTER THE MOMENT

A red eye flight later Eva stepped off the plane at Heathrow with little more than salted nuts and black coffee in her system. But she felt invigorated, if not outright ecstatic. Maybe it was from her sexual high in Vienna.

im here

do u want 2 cum over tn

She took a taxi to the same hotel in London where she first met Aabel. She freshened up after checking in. There was still plenty of time before night fell. She checked *Bangly,* but just out of habit. She read online about what exhibitions were up in London. But nothing tempted her. So Eva slipped into her black bikini and hit the rooftop pool.

The pool was empty. She dropped her towel onto a lounge chair and stepped up to the edge of the pool. She dived in head-first, savoring the sting of the cold water on her skin. She always loved that feeling of her body being overwhelmed by sensation.

Eva swam to the other end of the pool. As she was about the climb out, some-one stepped into the water where she had dived in. His dark brown skin glistened in the dim warm pool light as he disappeared under the water's surface. But not before she glimpsed his muscular build and the bulging package underneath his Speedos.

Was he semi-hard?

Is he just that big?

Is it even a cock?

What if it's some new waterproof pocket in swim trunks for your phone?

She decided not to get out of the pool. She clung to the edge, remaining under the water up to her shoulders so she could quietly watch as the man floated on his back at the other end. He seemed oblivious to her presence, even in her bikini, which naturally turned her on even more. As she watched him, Eva slipped a hand under her bikini bottom and found what she was looking for. Starting in a circular motion with her fingertips, she slowly rubbed her clit underwater. She let out a breathy moan as she played with herself. The water around her began to ripple outward in the same pleasing rhythm.

Eva could feel herself steadily building up to a climax. In a feat of self-control that surprised even her, she took another deep breath and pulled her hand out of her bikini bottom.

She wanted to wait.

She wanted Aabel.

Eva steeled herself and climbed out of the pool. She looked back before leaving and caught the man smiling at her.

Does he know what I was doing in the water?

Do I care?

She toweled off in her room and slipped into a black pencil skirt and her favorite torn Blondie t-shirt.

As night fell she walked out of the hotel and headed for Aabel's flat. The streets were slick and shiny from the light rain. But nothing could dampen Eva's mood.

She rang the buzzer and heard the front door of the building unlock. She walked up the stairs and knocked on Aabel's door. Time stood still while she waited. She checked her neckline to make sure the proper amount of cleavage was showing.

The door finally opened. Aabel stood there with a crooked smile. He leaned in to hug her, but they didn't kiss like she thought they would.

Aabel sat her down on the couch and offered her a glass of water. Eva grinned.

"Not in the mood for water."

Aabel sat down next to her. "Hey, we

need to talk."

He said he met someone else.

It just happened.

They weren't exclusive yet, so he was down to fuck, but he needed Eva to be cool about it. Was she cool? He figured it wouldn't be a big deal, since she was going back to New York soon, but he wanted to be honest.

Honesty was very important to him.

He leaned in close and whispered, "I'm glad you came." His breath reeked of cheap mouthwash.

Eva looked him in the eyes. She wanted to say, "You can do whatever you want." And she meant it. Her heart, body, mind, pussy were all his. To care about something or someone without an ounce of regret was one of the things Eva learned from Promises. And she wanted to practice what was preached. There was nothing she wouldn't give to him, fully and completely. She was his.

But instead, she said what was actually on her mind.

"I'm glad I'm leaving."

Eva got up and walked out the door.

After leaving Aabel's building and walking a few blocks, she stopped and pulled out her phone. She scrolled to the first text he ever sent her.

Now u have mine

Eva took a deep breath. She knew what she had to do. She tapped on her phone and deleted him.

Eva walked back to her hotel in the rain. She was soaking wet when she entered her room. She sat at the edge of the bed, trying to process what had just happened. She wasn't despondent or melancholic, which was surprising, all things considered. But what shocked Eva most was that she had enough wits to reflect on her feelings, instead of merely reacting to events. She felt that she had a say over what she felt, and what she wanted.

Something slowly came over her. It was an emotion that she hadn't expected. It welled up from out of nowhere and felt like the arrival of a kind stranger. The feeling was elation.

She jumped out of her damp skirt and panties but left her t-shirt on and wrapped a short towel around her that barely covered her ass. Then she headed for the rooftop.

When she stepped out of the elevator

Eva saw that the same man who was in the pool was still there in the water, with his arms out and legs close together, floating like a human cross. He had the most serene smile on his face.

She dropped her towel at the edge of the pool and dived into the cold water with her t-shirt on. Eva swam to the bottom and stayed there. She looked up at the man floating above her as he slowly glided across the pool. The eerie glow of the pool lights made it look like there was a strange halo around him. She relaxed her arms, letting them gently drift in the water.

At that moment, Eva felt sublimely peaceful. Maybe more peaceful than she had ever been. Her mind was at ease and yet alert at the same time. She wanted the moment to go on forever.

She exhaled and closed her eyes.

One.

Two.

Let it go.

Three.

Four.

Let it…

Water rushed into her lungs. Eva panicked. She pushed off from the bottom of the pool and swam to the surface, gasping for breath. She grabbed onto the edge of the pool and violently coughed up the water she had swallowed, trying to force air back into her system.

She felt like shit. But she was breathing. She closed her eyes and let out a sigh of relief.

Her moment had passed.

Eva then felt a hand on her shoulder. She opened her eyes. It was the man in the pool.

"You okay?" he asked.

"Guess I can't cut it as a mermaid," Eva replied.

"Don't mermaids seduce sailors and fuck them until they die?" he asked.

She caught him looking at her wet t-shirt.

"Those are sirens."

He flashed an easygoing smile.

Eva reached out and flirtatiously stroked his beard.

"And not only sailors," she said.

Eva watched as he sank below the surface. When he grabbed her feet she wondered what he was up to. Suddenly she felt his tongue on her toes under the water. It felt strange yet pleasing, and as she eased into it, began to enjoy it more. He moved up her body, gently kissing her legs and pelvis as Eva started to caress her own erect nipples underneath her t-shirt.

She could feel her body heat rising as his mouth reached her deep dark plum. He spread the folds of her pussy and pushed his tongue inside her, encircling her hidden pearl with gentle devotion.

A little worried about how long he was staying under the water, she tapped on his shoulder. But he didn't stop. In fact, he began to lick with more intensity. Eva looked up and gasped with pleasure as she spread her legs wider.

"God, I don't even know your name."

THE END

ABOUT THE AUTHOR

Photo by Katrín Inga Jónsdóttir Hjördísardóttir

Andrea McGinty is an artist and writer living and working in New York. She was born in 1985 in Sunrise, Florida. Andrea is fascinated by the way language can subtly reflect our societal conditions when filtered through intimate relationships. She received her MFA in Fine Arts from the School of Visual Arts in New York. Andrea has exhibited both nationally and internationally.

God, I Don't Even Know Your Name
is available as an enhanced ebook
with additional multimedia content for
Apple iBooks and Amazon Kindle.

For more information, visit
www.badlandsunlimited.com

Why Hang
When You Can